☆ Ghostyshocks ☆ Snow White ☆ Cinderboy ☆ Eco-Wolf ☆
☆ The Greedy Farmer ☆ Billy Beast ☆

DAFT JACK and the BEAN STACK

Daft Jack and his mother were so poor...

...they lived under a cow in a field. His mum slept at the front end...

...and Jack slept at the udder end.

Daisy was a good cow, but the problem was, Jack's mum was fed up with milk. It was all they ever had -
hot milk,
cold milk,
warm milk,
milk on toast,
milk pudding.

And on Sundays, for a special treat, they had Milk Surprise (which was really just milk with milk on top).

Jack didn't mind milk, but his mother would have given anything for a change.

"I'M SICK AND TIRED OF MILK!" she would shout. "If I never taste another drop as long as I live it will be too soon. If only you were a clever boy, Jack, you would think of something."

"I have thought of something," said Jack. "It's a new kind of milkshake - it's milk flavoured."

Jack's mum chased him all around the field.

One day, a terrible thing happened; Jack was sitting in the field eating a Mini Milk lolly and his mum was having her after-milk rest when Daisy suddenly looked up at the grey sky, decided it was going to rain and, as all cows do, lay down.

"Right! That is it. I've had enough!" spluttered Jack's mum when Jack had pulled her out by the ankles. "You will have to take Daisy into town and sell her. But make sure you get a good price or I'll chase you around the field for a week."

Daft Jack was very sad because Daisy was more like a friend than just a roof over his head. But he always liked to please his mother.

He made himself a milk sandwich for the journey and Jack and Daisy set off towards the town. It was a long way so they took it in turns to carry each other.

Then at the top of a hill, they met an old man sitting on a tree stump with a shopping bag.

"That's a fine cow you're carrying," he said. "What's your name, sonny?"

"It's Jack," said Jack, "but everyone calls me 'Daft', I don't know why."

"Well, Jack," said the old man. "I'd like to buy that cow from you."

“I would like to sell this cow too,” said Jack, “but you’ll have to give me a good price for her. Otherwise my mum will chase me around the field for a week.”

"I can see you're a clever boy," said the old man, "and I'm in a good mood today. So guess what I'm going to give you for that cow?"

"What?" said Jack.

The old man reached into his shopping bag.

"Beans!" said the old man. "Not just one bean! Not just two beans! I'm going to give you A WHOLE TIN OF BAKED BEANS".

Jack couldn't believe his luck. Not one bean, not two beans, but a WHOLE TIN of baked beans for just one old cow. It must have been his lucky day. At last his mum would be proud of him.

So Jack kissed Daisy goodbye and set off home carrying the tin of beans as carefully as he would carry a new born baby, feeling very pleased with himself.

As soon as he saw the field he began to shout, "Look Mum! All our troubles are over. Guess what I got for Daisy? Not one bean. Not two beans. But A WHOLE TIN COMPLETELY FULL OF BEANS! Why, mother there must be A HUNDRED yummy beans in this tin, I knew you'd be pleased."

At the end of the week,
when his mum had
finished chasing him,
Daft Jack and his mum
sat down in the
middle of the field.

"Oh Jack," wailed his mum. "Now we haven't even got a cow to sleep under. If only you were a clever boy, you'd think of something."

"I have thought of something, Mum," said Jack. "Let's eat the beans."

So Daft Jack and his mum ate the beans. Then they had nothing left at all.

That night, Jack couldn't sleep. "I can't do anything right," he thought sadly. "My poor Mother would be better off without me. I think I will run away into the big wide world and seek my fortune."

So Jack decided to leave a note for his mother. He couldn't find any paper so he tore the label from the bean tin. But there was something already written on the back of the baked bean label.

Jack held the paper up to the moonlight and read aloud...

Jack woke his mother. When she saw the message on the bean tin, she couldn't believe her eyes. "Oh Jack!" she cried. "At last we will be able to buy a proper house."

"Yes," said Jack, "and I will buy poor Daisy back. I fancy a nice glass of milk."

And Jack's mum was too happy to chase him around the field.

In the morning they sent off the lucky bean label and soon their prize arrived - A WHOLE LORRY LOAD OF BAKED BEANS.

Jack and his mum didn't know what to say. They began to stack the tins in one corner of the field, but before they had finished a second lorry load of beans arrived.

And all day long the lorries kept coming.

By the evening there was a huge pile of bean tins. A STACK of bean tins. A COLOSSAL GLEAMING MONUMENTAL MOUNTAIN of bean tins. There were bean tins right up to the clouds.

So from that day Daft Jack and his mum ate beans. It was all they ever had -
hot beans,
cold beans,
warm beans,
beans on toast,
bean pudding.

And on Sundays, for a special treat, they had Bean Surprise (which was really just beans with beans on top).

Jack's mum would have given anything for a change.

"I'm SICK AND TIRED OF BEANS!" she shouted one day. "If I never eat another bean as long as I live it will be too soon. If only you were a clever boy, Jack, you would think of something."

"I have thought of something," said Jack. "Bean juice milkshake."

There wasn't room to chase Jack around the field because the bean stack was too big. So Jack's mum chased him up the bean stack instead.

Higher and higher, Jack hopped from tin to tin with his mum puffing and panting behind.

Until at last Jack climbed so high he left his mum far behind. But Jack didn't stop. He kept on climbing. He looked down at the world below. He saw the field as small as a handkerchief and his mum as tiny as an ant. And still Jack climbed higher.

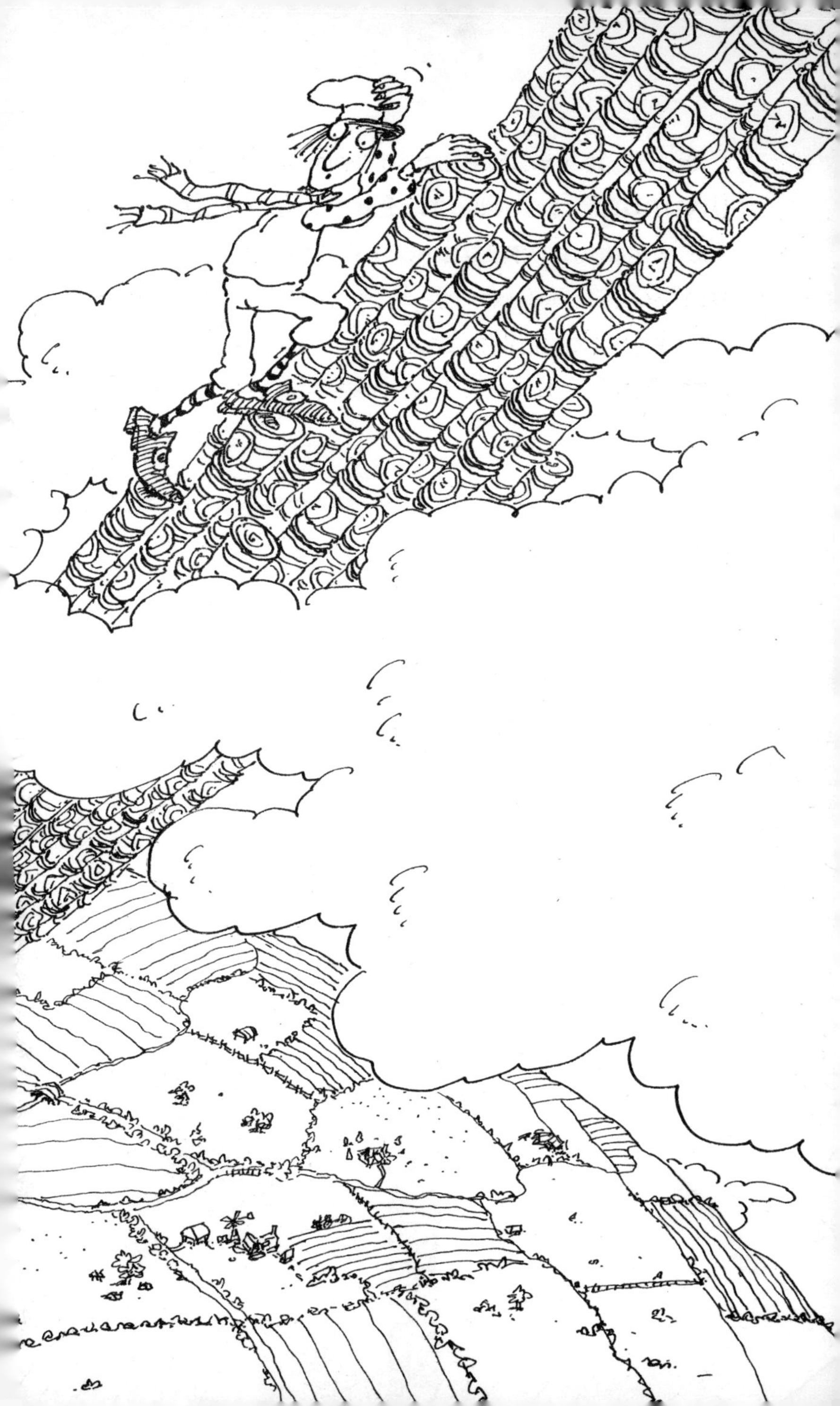

When he was almost too tired to climb any more, Jack reached the top of the bean stack, way up in the clouds.

Jack looked around. To his amazement he saw an enormous castle with its great door wide open.

He tiptoed inside. It was the most incredible place he had ever seen.

Jack wandered from room to room. He found massive bedrooms with carpets as thick as snow drifts, a solar heated Jacuzzi, a living room with great armchairs and a TV screen the size of a cinema.

At last, Jack wandered into a wonderful kitchen fitted with every kind of gadget.

Jack was interested in cooking and he climbed up to took at the giant sized microwave.

Suddenly, the whole castle began to shake. A great voice roared.

FEE, FI, FO, FUM,
I'VE GOT A GIANT PAIN IN MY TUM!

Jack looked around in alarm and saw an enormous giant sitting at a table, rubbing his stomach and looking very miserable.

"'S not fair!" complained the giant. "All I ever get to eat is CHILDREN! And now I've got a belly ache...

Hot kids,
cold kids,
warm kids,
kids on toast,
kid pudding.
And on Sundays,
for a special treat,
I have Kid Surprise
(but that's just kids
with kids on top).
I'd give ANYTHING for a change. I'M SICK AND TIRED OF KIDS! If I never ate another kid as long as I live it would be too soon..."
He looked down at Jack. "AND NOW I'VE GOT TO EAT YOU TOO! S' NOT FAIR!"

The giant reached out a huge hairy hand and grabbed Jack around the waist.

He lifted Jack kicking and struggling into the air and opened his vast black cave-like mouth with a tongue like a huge purple carpet.

"Well," thought Jack, "this is the end of Daft Jack and no mistake."

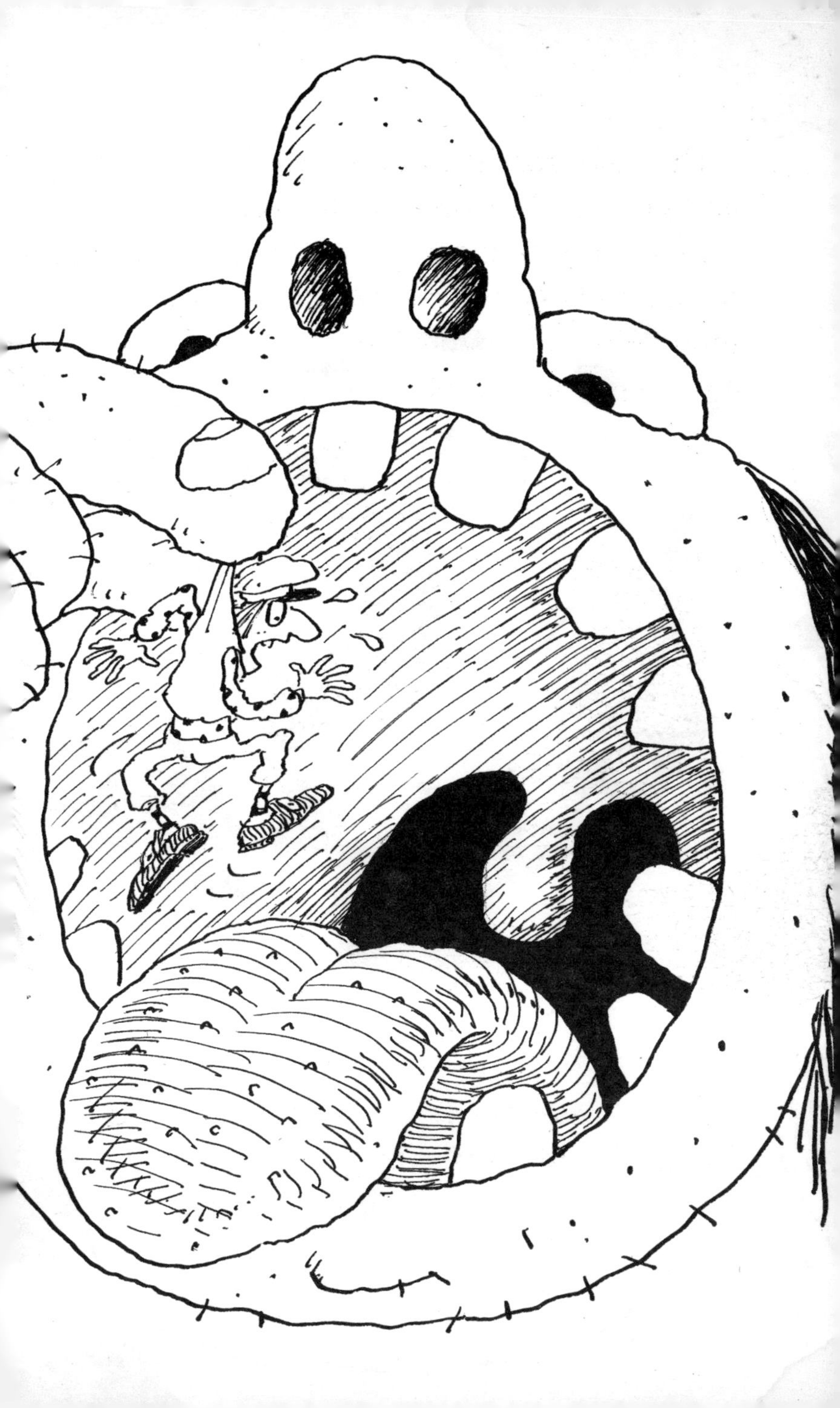

He was just about to be crunched into a million tiny daft pieces, when suddenly he had an idea.

"Er, Excuse me, Mr Giant," he whispered nervously. "If you eat me it will only make your tummy ache worse. I can think of something much nicer. I don't suppose you like...beans do you?"

"BEANS!" roared the giant "DO I LIKE BEANS? I YUMMY YUMMY LOVE 'em!"

So Jack took the giant by the hand and led him down the bean stack. And on the way, the giant told Jack how lonely he was, all by himself in the great big castle in the clouds with nothing to do but eat people.

Jack began to feel very sorry for the poor giant and took him home to meet his mum.

"Oh Jack," she cried. "Where ever have you bean?"

Jack's mum was very pleased to see Jack in one piece. But when she saw the giant...!

And when the giant saw Jack's mum...!

It was love at first sight.

FEE, FI, FO, FUM,
I'M GOING TO MARRY
DAFT JACK'S MUM!

"Of course you are, dear," said Jack's mum, "but first you must be hungry after your long journey."

The giant looked at the bean stack, gleaming in the evening light as he licked his giant lips.

He began munching the beans. Not one tin, not two tins, but the whole stack of beans. And he didn't even stop to open the tins.

So Daft Jack's mum married the giant, and they were very happy. They all went to live in the giant's wonderful castle in the sky.

Daft Jack opened a cafe in the giant's kitchen and he called it 'DAFT JACK'S SKY SNACKS'. And people came from far and wide and Jack grew rich and happy.

He served everything you can think of except milk...

and beans!

SHAMPOOZEL

There was once a jolly hairdresser named Dan Druff.

Dan LOVED hair!

Curly hair and bristly hair, eyebrows and beards – Dan loved them all. He loved the gleam of his many mirrors and the snippety-snick of sparkling silver scissors.

Dan even sang about hair.

Hair, hair, glorious hair,
It spreads from your head,
Nearly EVERYWHERE.

It grows on your toes,
Even inside your nose,
Hair, hair, HA-A-A-I-I-R!!

Only one thing upset Dan's happiness – his girlfriend, Tam O'Tei, who lived in the flat upstairs.

Unlike Dan, Tam was a sad person who hid away in her bedroom behind tightly drawn curtains. From under their hairdryers, Dan's customers could hear her wretched moans and Dan nearly tore his hair out with worry over her condition.

The awful truth was . . .

. . . Tam O'Tei had terrible hair!

"Oh, Dan," she wailed. "My head is dull and lifeless. I have a flaky scalp and unsightly split ends, but no ordinary shampoo is effective."

Dan could find nothing to help, and as the days passed, Tam's hair grew as greasy as a chip-shop mop.

Now, not far from the barber shop was an evil black tower which twisted into the sky like a strange hairstyle.

This was the home of the Bad Hair Witch.

High in her dark rooms, the Bad Hair Witch mixed strange shampoos and hair oils which were sold all over the world. The secret ingredients came from rare plants which grew only in her private garden.

Above the barber shop, Tam became convinced that one of these magical hair herbs would bring life back to her dull scalp and she pleaded with Dan to pick some.

At the mention of the black tower, Dan Druff felt the hairs prickle at the back of his neck.

"I dare not go there," he whispered. "What if I should fall into the evil hairgrip of the Bad Hair Witch?"

But Tam O'Tei complained so long and hard that at last Dan Druff could stand it no longer. "All right, keep your hair on," he bristled. "I will go to the tower and comb the gardens for your herbs."

So the next morning, before dawn, the brave barber crept reluctantly up the hairpin bends that led to the tower.

As he walked, he sang to keep up his courage.

Before he could finish his song, Dan had almost walked into a huge sign hanging on the wall before him:

DAN DRUFF
USE YOUR HEAD
IF YOU CLIMB THIS
WALL,
YOU'LL WISH YOU
WERE DEAD

Dan felt a shiver run along his moustache. Only the thought of Tam's sad locks drove him on. Ignoring the sign, he scrambled into the Bad Hair Witch's secret garden where he found a second sign:

DAN DRUFF, CAN'T YOU READ?
DON'T EVEN THINK
ABOUT NICKING A WEED

Poor Dan had never been in such a hairy situation, but he bent down and began to stuff his pockets with the herbs.

Suddenly he heard a terrible voice:

"Dan Druff, you must be crazy,
You'll pay for those plants,
With your very first baby."

Dan's hair stood on end – it was the worst rhyme he had ever heard.

Before him stood . . . the Bad Hair Witch!

"B-but I don't have a b-baby," stammered Dan.

"Well, let's not split hairs," snapped the witch. "I will wait until your first child is born."

Grabbing a last handful of herbs, Dan leapt over the wall and hared down the hill to the town.

He found Tam in her bedroom wearing a paper bag on her head, and he poured out the story of his terrifying brush with the Bad Hair Witch.

But Tam was barely listening. She seized the wonderful herbs, crushed them and began to lather her scalp . . .

As if by magic, Tam's hair turned into a glorious mass of glossy curls which seemed to flow in slow motion when she tossed her head.

Tam O'Tei was cured!

She tore downstairs into the sunny shop, and, as Dan shaved the bristly early morning customers, Tam happily set to work beside him, sweeping up the fallen curls and locks.

That very week, Tam and Dan were married and the whole town joined them in this glorious hymn:

Before a year was out, the couple's happiness was complete – a beautiful baby daughter was born, and, after much thought, they called her…

In that happy hairy world, not one thought was given to the Bad Hair Witch.

But the Bad Hair Witch had forgotten nothing.

High in her tower she worked day and night on her most amazing invention yet – something all barbers dream of – a marvellous, magical HAIR GROWING LOTION!

"Guess which witch will be rich?" she sniggered. "All I need is a helpless, hairless baby to test my invention."

And so the Bad Hair Day dawned. The bell at the little barber shop tinkled cruelly as the Bad Hair Witch burst inside.

"Give me the child!" she shrieked.

"Have you got an appointment?" said Tam. "Let's see, I could fit you in on Thursday . . ."

"You don't understand, you fools. I need to test my new improved formula – Ultimate 2-in-1 Hair Growing Lotion."

"Leave Shampoozel alone," pleaded Tam O'Tei. "You cannot try out your hair-brained inventions on our child."

Ignoring the tears of the unfortunate couple, the Bad Hair Witch seized Shampoozel and carried her back to the tower.

To make sure the precious child would never be taken from her, the Hair Witch bricked up the front door behind them.

As the days passed, the Bad Hair Witch grew to love the baby and looked after her as if she were her own.

She would sing as she washed the infant's hair:

No more tears, Baby Shampoozel,
My magic shampoo is very unusual.

And day by day, as Shampoozel grew, her hair grew too, in great long golden tresses which tumbled across the floor, down the stairs, into the kitchen, under the dog, round the back of the fridge and back upstairs again.

"Hair, hair, HAIR!" cackled the Bad Hair Witch. "Look at all your beautiful golden hair!"

Sometimes hairy Shampoozel remembered her parents' little barber shop in the town far below.

Now that their daughter had gone, Dan and Tam worked sadly and never sang anymore; and so, one by one, the customers went elsewhere.

Years passed, and as Shampoozel grew into a young woman, the Bad Hair Witch taught her the secret art of the hairdresser:

Wash your hair and keep it sweet.
Lather, rinse, repeat.
Rub and comb and keep it neat.
Lather, rinse, repeat.

Together, the Bad Hair Witch and Shampoozel created new hair products which were more amazing than anyone could have dreamed of.

They became so famous, in fact, that a young prince by the name of Gary Baldie heard about them from his home in a distant land.

The prince, although handsome and wealthy, was as bald as a billiard ball.

Prince Gary had tried one wig-maker after another but without satisfaction so when he finally heard about Ultimate 2-in-1 Hair Growing Lotion, he set out straight away, and after many days arrived at the tower.

Of course, even a prince cannot enter a tower without a door. So Prince Gary concealed himself beneath the walls and after a while he saw an amazing thing.

The Bad Hair Witch appeared at the window with her shopping bag. All of a sudden a great mass of hair cascaded to the ground. The witch slid down it and set off towards the town.

"I suppose that's what they call a hair slide!" whispered Prince Gary in amazement.

Half an hour later, the old lady returned with her shopping and called out:

Shampoozel, Shampoozel,
Let down your hair,
So I can climb to the top
Of your long hairy stair.

Shampoozel let down her locks again and the old woman scrambled back up the tower.

Gary Baldie was no fool and the next time the old woman went out, the prince stood below the window himself and called:

Shampoozel, Shampoozel,
Your hair is so curly,
Let it hang down now,
Be a good girlie.

To his delight, a great coil of hair tumbled to the ground. He seized it and began to baldly go where no man had gone before.

The prince scrambled into Shampoozel's room, and when his royal eyes fell on the lovely Shampoozel he was captivated by her hairiness.

He leaned towards her and kissed her ruby red lips.

There and then, Shampoozel and the prince fell in love. Gary told her that he adored her limitless locks, and how he would love to have some of his own.

To his amazement, Shampoozel replied that she had grown tired of her hair. "It don't half hurt when people climb up it," she complained. "And it takes a week to wash."

But then, to the prince's joy, Shampoozel pulled out a tiny bottle of Ultimate 2-in-1 Hair Growing Lotion and began to massage his shiny scalp. Almost immediately, a single hair popped out of the prince's head.

The first hair was followed by a second, the second by a third, and within ten minutes the prince had a mass of golden curls snaking down his back, nearly as long as Shampoozel's.

Gary Baldie seized Shampoozel and danced with joy.

"My prince, you must wash and go," whispered Shampoozel.

She brushed a few stray hairs from his collar, and with one final kiss, the prince climbed down Shampoozel's hair and slipped away into the shadows.

It wasn't long before the Bad Hair Witch returned.

Shampoozel, Shampoozel,
Don't make me shout,
Let down your hair, Girl,
Don't hang about.

As soon as she entered the salon, the witch spotted Gary Baldie's little crown, which Shampoozel had left hanging on the coat hook.

The witch was furious and, after a terrible argument, stormed into her bedroom, leaving Shampoozel weeping pitifully.

The prince, meanwhile, had decided that witch or no witch, he had to see Shampoozel again. He stood at the foot of the tower and whispered:

Shampoozel, Shampoozel,
Here is your prince,
Throw down your pigtail,
My hair needs a rinse.

Immediately, a long lock of hair curled out of the window and tumbled to the ground.

But just as the prince was about climb up, he saw a figure sliding down . . .

It was Shampoozel!

"I don't know why I didn't think of this before," she said. "All that stupid hair. I snipped it off and tied it to the bed. Then I slid down to you. At last we have escaped from the Bad Hair Witch."

"That was a close shave!" replied Gary Baldie, softly stroking her silky stubble. "Come on, let's really let our hair down."

So Shampoozel and her hairy prince ran away to his castle, but she didn't forget her parents, Dan Druff and Tam O'Tei.

Although they were rich, Shampoozel and Gary Baldie liked to work in Dan's shop on Saturdays.

Before long, the little barber-shop was once again the busiest in the land.

"It's amazing how the customers keep coming back," laughed Dan.

And it was true – some of the customers seemed to have as many as five haircuts a day.

Perhaps they just loved having their hair cut by Shampoozel.

Or perhaps the secret shampoo she uses has something to do with it . . .

Or perhaps they come for the endless happy songs which drift across the hairy town . . .

High in her tower, even the Bad Hair Witch joins in:

Hair, hair, SENSATIONAL hair,
Shampoozel's the girl,
To share your hair care.
She can give you a shave,
Or a permanent wa-a-ve,
Hair, HAIR...
H-A-A-A-A-I-I-I-R-R-R!!!!

ECO-WOLF and the THREE PIGS

In a small wigwam in a beautiful valley lived a gentle creature called Eco-Wolf.

There were no cars or houses in the valley, and Eco-Wolf lived at peace with the trees and the wild animals. He spent his time inventing machines which would make electricity from the clear blue river without causing pollution.

One morning, Eco-Wolf was gently explaining to a young animal about litter.

As they spoke, a huge black car roared into the valley. Out climbed three sinister figures dressed in black. The biggest pig stepped forward:

We're the three pigs and we are BAD,
Greedypig, Grabbit and Megadad.
We don't hang about or dilly-dally,
We're gonna build houses in your valley.
So don't get smart, don't no one get funny,
The pigs are out to make some money.

COMING
SOON
LUXURY
HOMES
Enquiries to
Pigsty Properties PLC

Eco-Wolf couldn't believe what he was hearing.

"Hey, man," he said, "your car is, like, invading my space. You're messing up the valley vibes, piggy brother."

But the pigs only laughed and set to work.

They built a big, ugly straw cottage beside the river, with a huge satellite dish on the roof. They had to cut down one or two old oak trees that were in the way, but the pigs didn't care about trees.

As they worked the pigs sang very loudly:

Who's afraid of this eco-guy?
If we messed his hair, he'd be sure to cry.

This valley ain't so peaceful no more,
House number one is made of straw.

We're the three pigs, we don't care a fig,
Megadad, Grabbit and Greedypig.

When they had finished, the pigs put up a 'For Sale' sign and went inside to eat a HUGE meal.

Eco-Wolf was very sad to see a house beside the blue river, but he was especially sad about the old oak trees. He called the wild animals to his wigwam.

"Hey, wild warrior brother-sisters," said Eco-Wolf. "I don't dig these big pigs. Those trees were kind of like my sister-brothers too. It makes me huff and puff, man."

So Eco-Wolf and his friends walked up to the door of the straw cottage and rang the bell.

"Big Pig, Big Pig," said Eco-Wolf, "like, let me come in."

"Get outa here, buddy," shouted Megadad, "or you'll get a piggy-punch on your chinny-chin-chin."

"Then we'll, like, huff and puff, man, and blow your house sky high," replied Eco-Wolf.

Out of the air came all the wild birds of the valley. They carried away every last piece of straw in their beaks, leaving Greedypig, Grabbit and Megadad with nothing but their TV set.

“That’s the last straw. Right, boys?” said Megadad.

Peace returned to the valley. Eco-Wolf went back to his Eco-Power machine, and the clear river flowed.

But the three bad pigs were making another plan.

"Gather round, boys," said Megadad. "That straw house was a lousy idea. We gotta make somethin' a WHOLE LOT tougher to keep out this Eco-Wolf fella. Right, boys?"

So the bad pigs started work on a wooden house. It had six bedrooms with double-glazed windows, a garage, a swimming pool and a road leading up to it.

The pigs had to dig up some wild flowers and chase a few rabbits out of their homes, but they didn't care about flowers or rabbits.

While they worked, the three pigs sang even louder:

So who's afraid of this eco-freak?
He's a sneaky geek with a whole lotta cheek.

We'll flatten this valley and do it good,
House number two is made of wood.

We're the three pigs, so goodbye rabbit,
Greedypig, Megadad and brother Grabbit.

When they had finished, the three pigs put up a 'For Sale' sign and went inside to eat a COLOSSAL meal.

Eco-Wolf was very sad to see another house in the valley, but he was especially sad about the rabbits. He called the wild animals to his wigwam.

"Hey, wild warrior brother-sisters," said Eco-Wolf, "these big pigs are totally uncool. Those rabbits were kind of like my sister-brothers. It makes me huff and puff, man."

So Eco-Wolf and the woodland warriors marched up to the wooden house and rang the bell.

"Big Pig, Big Pig," said Eco-Wolf, "like, let me come in."

"Get outa here, buddy," shouted Megadad, "or you'll get a chop on your chinny-chin-chin."

"Then we'll, like, huff and puff, man, and blow your house into the middle of next week," replied Eco-Wolf.

Out of the fields came all the underground animals of the valley. They dug tunnels deep under the wooden house until it collapsed, leaving the three pigs in a pile of sawdust.

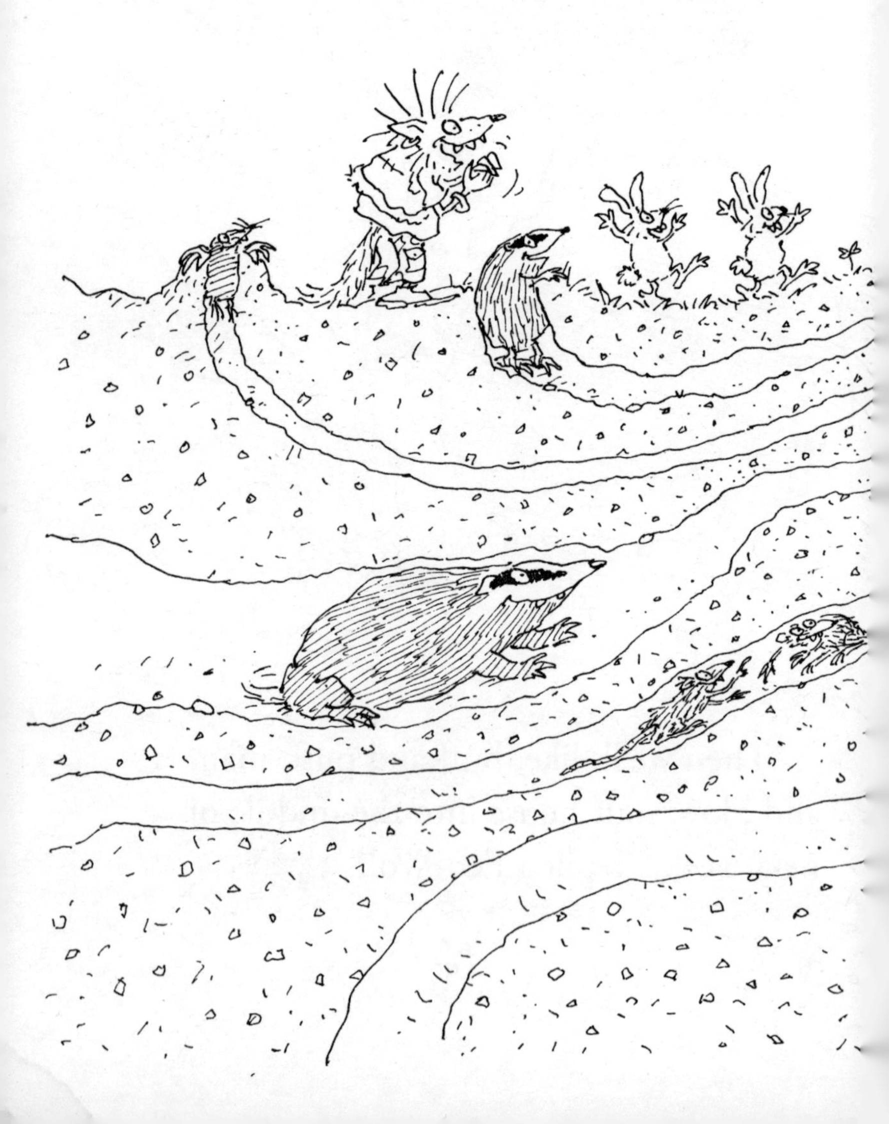

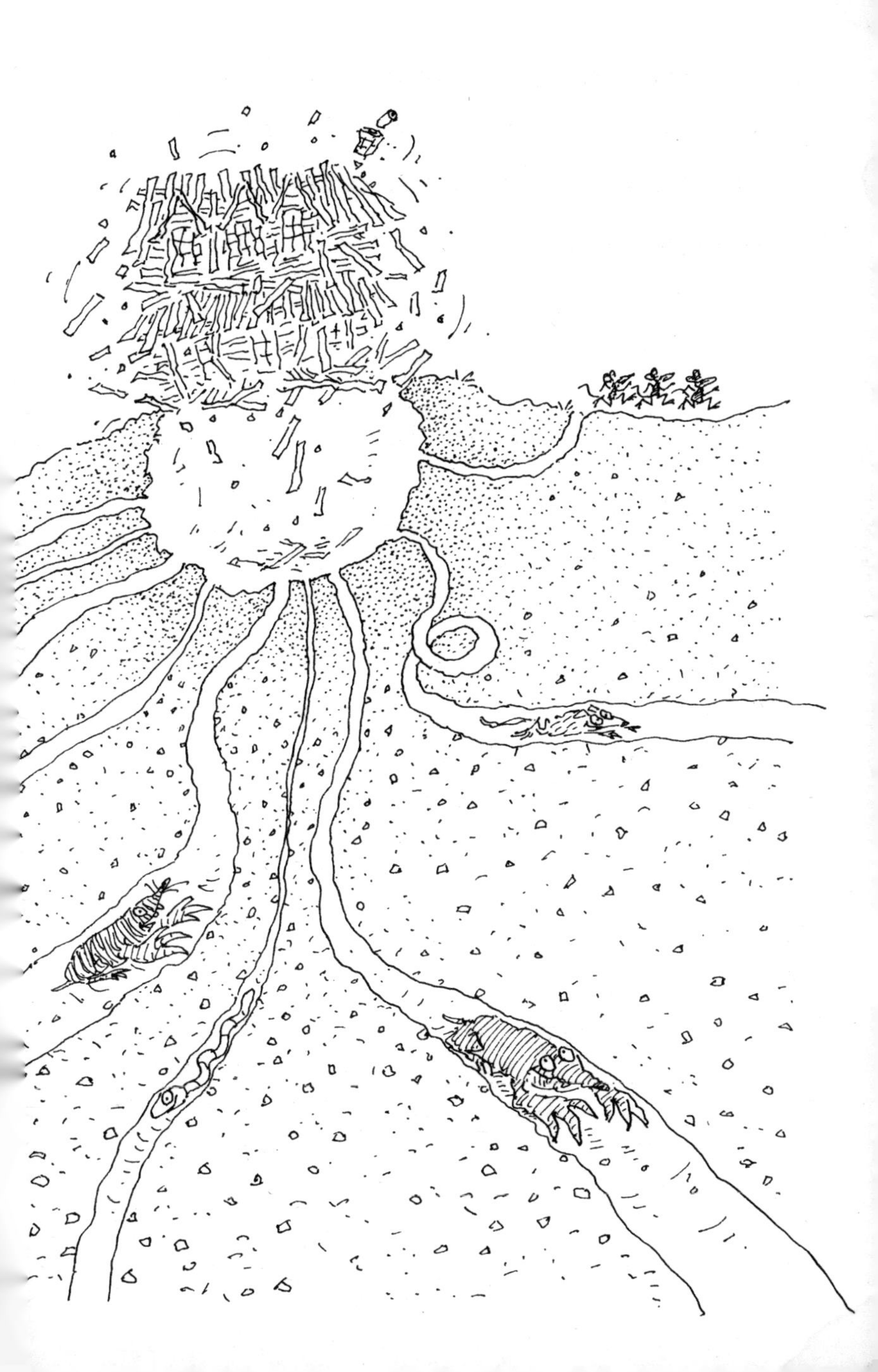

Peace returned once more to the valley. Eco-Wolf went back to his Eco-Power machine and the blue river flowed.

But the three bad pigs were making an even bigger plan.

“Gather round, boys. That wooden house was a lousy idea. We gotta make somethin’ a WHOLE LOT tougher to keep out this Eco-Wolf guy. Right, boys?”

So the bad pigs started work again. This time they used bricks and concrete. They built a high-rise tower block on top of a multi-storey shopping centre, with a motorway leading up to it.

They needed a lot of electricity, so the three pigs built a huge power station, with a gigantic chimney, right in the middle of the valley.

They had to cut down a forest, and the waste from the power station polluted the river, but the pigs didn't care about forests or rivers.

While they worked the three pigs sang more loudly than ever:

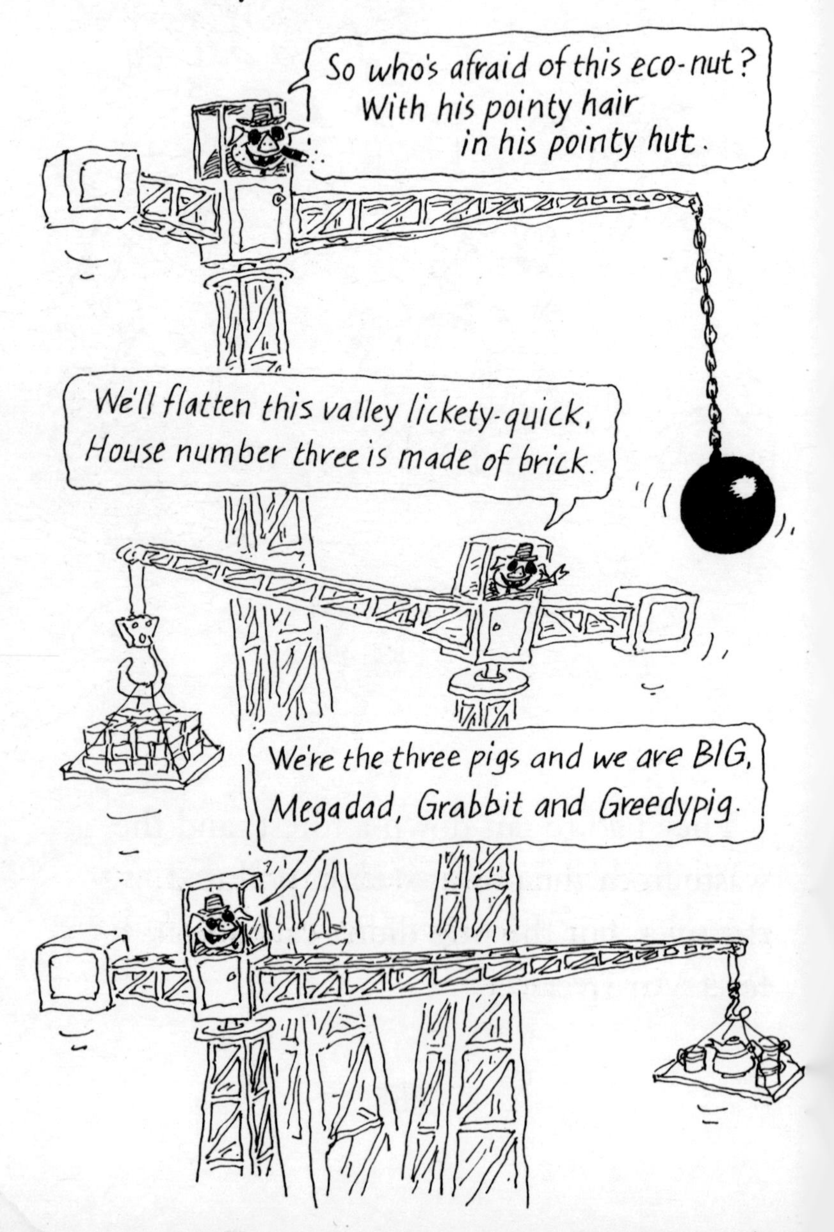

When they had finished, the three pigs put up a 'For Sale' sign and went inside to eat a MEGA meal.

Eco-Wolf looked at the remains of his beautiful valley. The river was grey, and the air was black and smoky.

“Hey, wild warrior brother-sisters,” he said, “this valley was, like, my sister-brother, man. It makes me mad. It makes me ballistic. It makes me HUFF and PUFF, man.”

Eco-Wolf and the wild woodland warriors stormed up to the power station. There was a big barbed wire fence all around.

Eco-Wolf pressed the button on the entry-phone.

"Big Pig, Big Pig," he said, "like, let me come in."

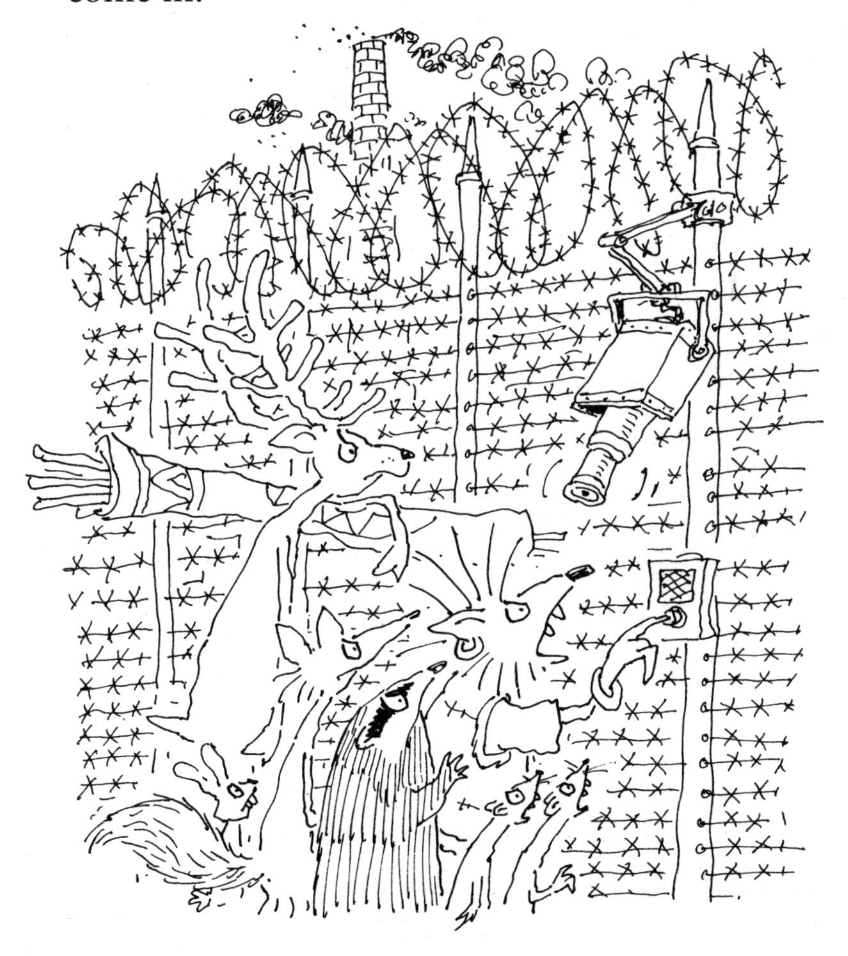

"Clear off, or I'll send out the security guards to give you a knuckle sandwich on your chinny-chin-chin," came Megadad's voice.

"Then I'll, like, huff and puff, man, and blow you and your power station into pork scratchings," replied Eco-Wolf.

Deep inside the power station, the three pigs only laughed.

"Hey, wild warriors," said Eco-Wolf, "I'm gonna climb that chimney stack and, like, camp on top, until those big pigs start respecting the planet."

Eco-Wolf strapped his wigwam on to his back. The warrior squirrels scrambled up the fence and pulled Eco-Wolf after them. He began to climb the chimney. It was very high, but Eco-Wolf was brave.

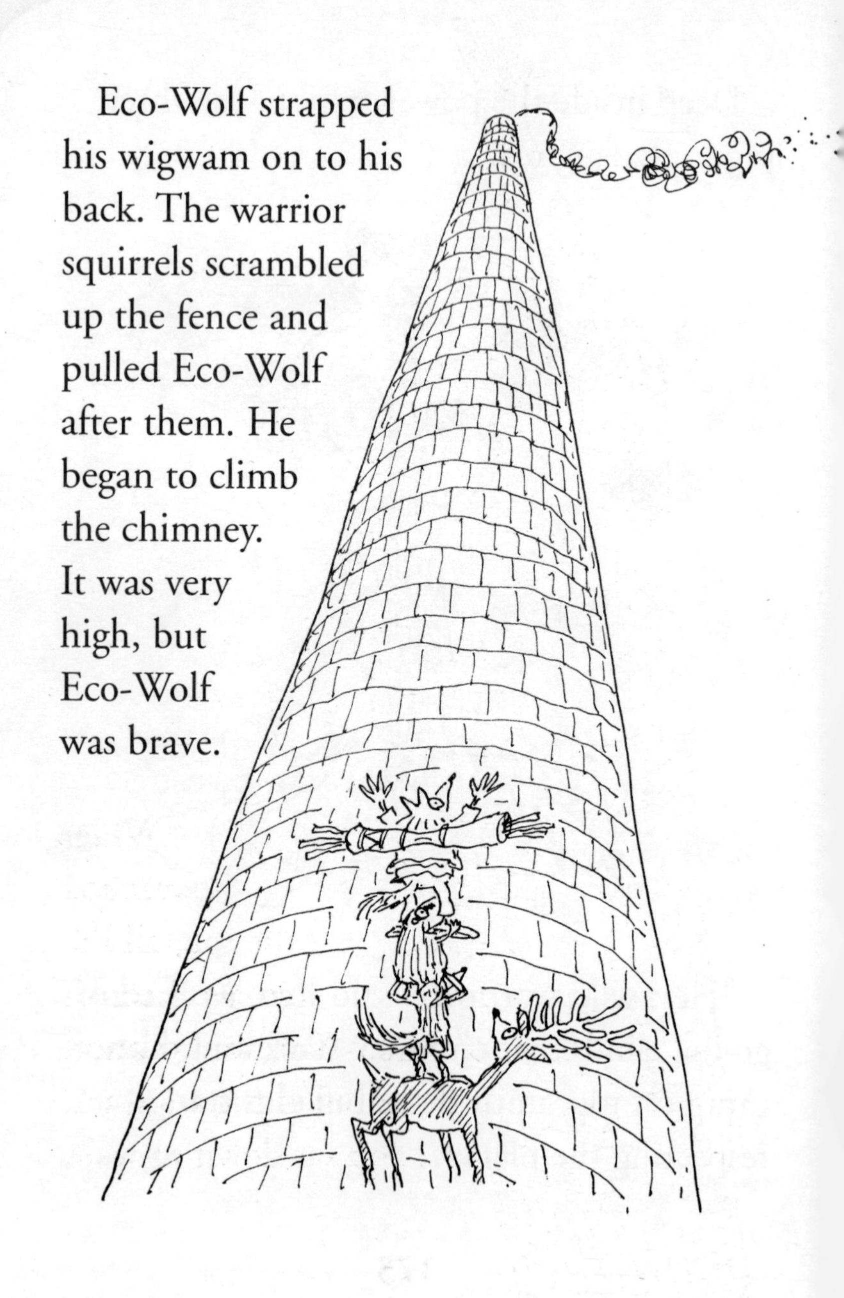

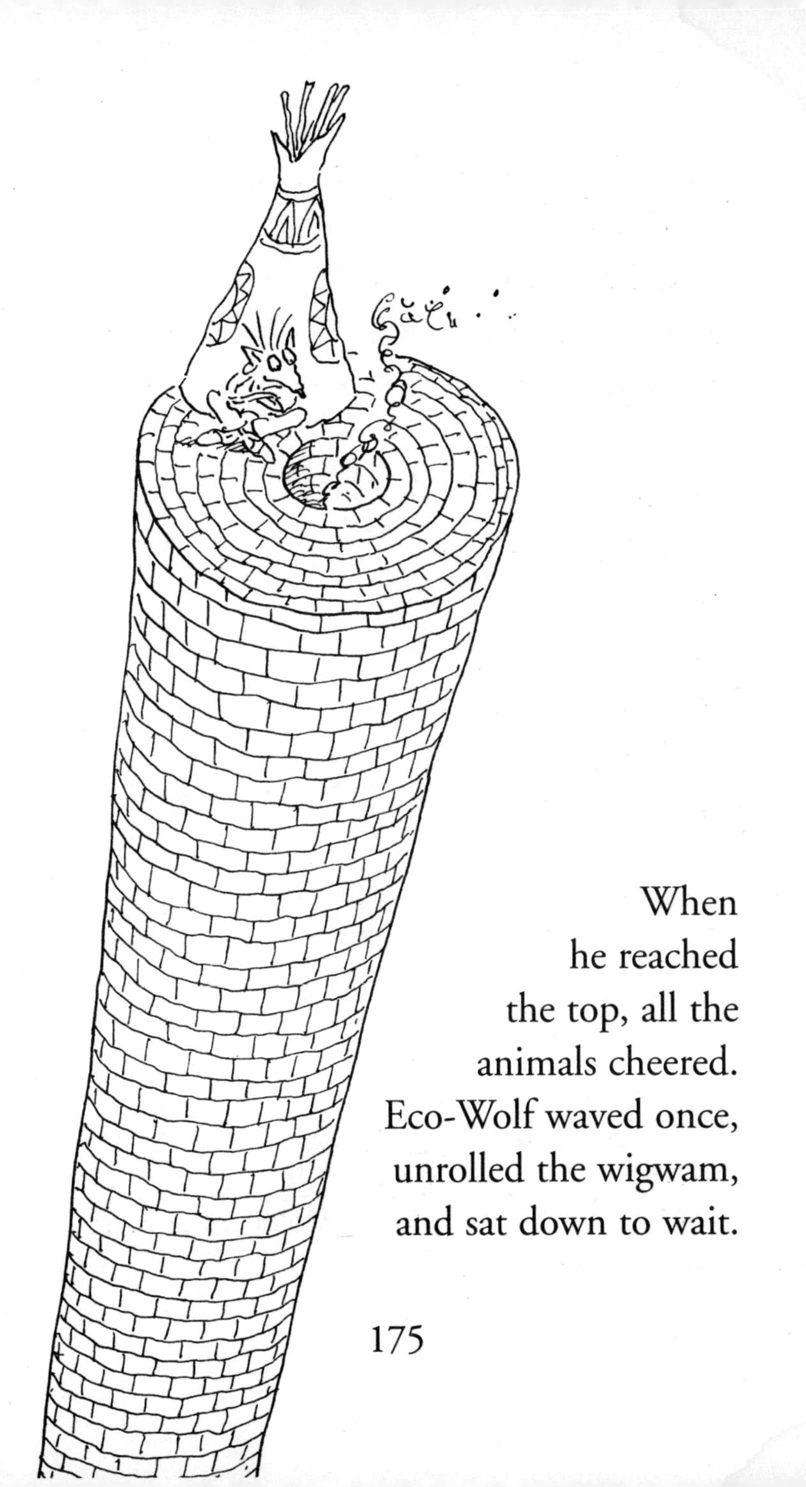

When
he reached
the top, all the
animals cheered.
Eco-Wolf waved once,
unrolled the wigwam,
and sat down to wait.

"OK, guys. We'll smoke that wolf out," said Megadad. "Right, boys?"

"Right, Dad," replied Greedypig and Grabbit, pulling a lever which turned the station to maximum power.

The heat in the power station started to build up. Black smoke poured out of the chimney.

Quick as a flash, Eco-Wolf pulled his wigwam over the top of the chimney so that the smoke drifted back down to the three pigs.

"I'll go up and get him, Dad," coughed Greedypig.

He climbed up inside the chimney, but, three-quarters of the way up, he got stuck.

"He's too fat," spluttered Grabbit. "I'll go up and get him, Dad."

So Grabbit climbed up inside the chimney, but, halfway up, he got stuck too.

"You're both too fat," shouted Megadad. "I'll go up and get him."

So Megadad climbed up inside the chimney, but, only a quarter of the way up, he got stuck too.

The chimney grew hotter and hotter. The three pigs began to squeal.

Suddenly, there was a huge explosion.

Eco-Wolf shot high into the air. Then, holding on to his wigwam like a parachute, he drifted gently to the ground. The three bad pigs were fired out of the chimney like piggy cannonballs.

Greedypig landed in the river.

Grabbit landed on the roof of the big black car.

And Megadad smashed right on to Eco-Wolf's eco-power machine.

The high-rise tower block and every one of Megadad's buildings exploded into a thousand tiny pieces.

"Like huff and puff, man. I blew that house down," said Eco-Wolf.

After many days, Eco-Wolf and the woodland warriors finished clearing up the valley. The three big pigs were made to plant new trees and dig new homes for the rabbits.

While they worked the three pigs sang very quietly:

We're a little bit afraid of this eco-bloke,
Who turned our houses into smoke.

We'll tidy the valley and do our best,
To let Mother Nature do the rest.

We're the three pigs and we are sad,
Grabbit, Greedypig and Megadad.

When they had finished, the three pigs climbed into their car, drove out of the valley and far, far away.

At last, the blue river flowed, and the air was clean again. A young animal asked Eco-Wolf how he would make electricity now that his Eco-Water Power machine was broken.

Eco-Wolf smiled. He was already working on a new idea.

Billy Bonkers

**'Utterly bonkers!
A riot of fun! I loved it!'
– Harry Enfield**

Mad stuff happens with Billy Bonkers! Whether he's flying through the air propelled by porridge power, or blasting headfirst into a chocolate-covered planet – life is never boring with Billy, it's BONKERS!

Three hilarious stories in one from an award-winning author and illustrator team.

8 1 84616 151 3 £4.99 pbk

978 1 40830 357 3 £5.99 pbk

978 1 40831 465 4 £4.99 pbk

Max and Molly's Guide To Trouble!

Meet Max and Molly: terrorising the neighbourhood really extremely politely...

Max and Molly's guides guarantee brilliantly funny mayhem and mischief as we learn how to be a genius, catch a criminal, build an abominable snowman and stop a Viking invasion!

978 1 40830 519 5 £4.99 Pbk
978 1 40831 572 9 eBook

978 1 40830 520 1 £4.99 Pbk
978 1 40831 573 6 eBook

978 1 40830 521 8 £4.99 Pbk
978 1 408 31574 3 eBook

978 1 40830 522 5 £4.99 Pb
978 1 408 31575 0 eBook

ORCHARD BOOKS

www.orchardbooks.co.uk